WOMAN KILLER

By

Chiori Miyagawa

NoPassport Press
Dreaming the Americas Series

No Passport is a Pan-American theatre alliance & press devoted to live, virtual and print action, advocacy, and change toward the fostering of cross-cultural diversity in the arts with an emphasis on the embrace of the hemispheric spirit in US Latina/o and Latin-American theatremaking.

NoPassport Press' Theatre & Performance PlayTexts Series and its Dreaming the Americas Series promotes new writing for the stage, texts on theory and practice, and theatrical translations.

Series Editors:
Randy Gener, Jorge Huerta, Otis Ramsey-Zoe, Stephen Squibb, Caridad Svich

Advisory Board:
Daniel Banks, Amparo Garcia-Crow, Maria M. Delgado, Elana Greenfield, Christina Marin, Antonio Ocampo-Guzman, Sarah Cameron Sunde, Saviana Stanescu, Tamara Underiner, Patricia Ybarra

Contents

A Soul Raging and Homeless

Woman Killer premiered at HERE Arts Center in Lower Manhattan on September 6, 2001, only days before the 9/11 attack on the World Trade Center, and when it reopened, audiences could see and smell the smoke from the burning ashes that seemed to usher in the global war on terror. Violence and loss are at the heart of this play, and the resonance between onstage victims and those who had perished a few blocks away was not lost on the cast or audiences. Chiori Miyagawa's dramatic work, however, is not rooted in any specific set of conditions that give rise to vengeance and mayhem, targeting power brokers and sacrificing innocents. It was inspired by the 1721 bunraku (puppet) play by Chikamatsu Monzeamon about an oil merchant's son who, in a moment of desperation, murders the wife of a family friend in his frantic effort to steal money to pay his debts. Although Chikamatsu's domestic dramas (sewamono joruri) depicted actual incidents of the time, Miyagawa's play is not rooted in the topical. Her characters often experience multiple historical moments, even when depicted in a particular setting. Time becomes expansive or circular, and specific scenes repeat themselves as in a time loop. Historical consciousness emerges from the intersections of personal and collective memories that emanate from and yet transcend culture.

In her theatrical rendering of a young man's disastrous efforts to escape the confines of family, community and societal expectations, Miyagawa explores our fears of unfulfilled desires, loss, and mortality that haunt not only the disaffected among us, but also those whose lives are organized by notions of belonging and who find deep satisfaction in marital bonds and familial love. Although the conflict between elements that Chikamatsu scholars refer to as *giri* (duty, obligation) and *ninjo* (emotion) [1] might be framed with very different correlates in our postmodern age, it is not difficult to imagine a "soul raging and homeless," bent on self gratification at all costs and profoundly alienated by others' needs. Everyone in his path—lover, sister, parents and even confidantes, like Anne, the young wife and mother who befriends him—becomes an obstacle blocking his insatiable desire, a cauldron of "blue fire." As Clay tells his dutiful brother who tries "not to want": "I want so much, want so much, I can hardly stand it. It's blue, sharp clear icy blue, and so scorching hot it burns my eyes....I'm so thirsty I can taste my own death."

Chikamatsu's *Woman-Killer and the Hell of Oil* begins with the general contours of its genre—a young man of the merchant class falls in love with a courtesan and finds himself unable to possess her (perhaps buy her contract from her owner or detach himself from prior vows). Often the scenario ends in a double suicide of the lovers in the hope that some form of redemption will be attained in death. In the murder play, *Woman-Killer*, however, the protagonist Kohei is engulfed by other wants, and he eschews pleas from his family to attend to business responsibilities, religious pilgrimages, and filial duties. He is drawn into the pleasure quarters, the licensed district of courtesans and popular entertainments where upstanding young merchants and even the revered samurai could enter what Haruo Shirane calls an "intoxicating, out-of-the ordinary festival-like world where the line between reality and dream was blurred." Within this domain, "citizens' excess energy could be channeled and... it was understood that there would be no criticism of the existing order." [2] Unfortunately, Kohei is unable to observe these boundaries. Having dishonored his samurai uncle in a brawl, assaulted his parents, and forged notes to the money-lenders, he victimizes a young matron of his community who has shown him kindness and ultimately her vulnerability. Slashing her body from throat to waist, he slips and slides on spilled oil and flowing blood, like a "demon in hell."

In Chiori Miyagawa's *Woman-Killer*, set in contemporary Brooklyn, the protagonist Clay has far fewer restrictions on his behavior—no samurai code to uphold, no pilgrimages of the oil

9

merchant's guild, and no family honor which would impel him to commit suicide. However, like Yohei, who must decide where to escape from confrontation with his uncle, Clay feels trapped in his own evasions. Even as his friend James points out that he is at the crossroads of Brooklyn—his own universe "southeast to Nagasaki, northeast to Kyoto, southwest to Manhattan, northwest to the Temple Kanzeon," Clay resides in shadows and stalks his girlfriend, Rebecca, whose call-girl activities stoke his jealousy. For Clay there is no pleasure quarter, space of "controlled release (nagusami)" other than the rather tame Halloween evening, the "only time you can be something other than yourself without consequence of punishment." The result is the same: Clay murders James's wife Anne, and slips and slides in her blood, "caught in a cycle, doomed to suffer eternally in the flickering blazing hell."

Perhaps the most striking departure from the bunraku play in Miyagawa's dramatization of the profligate son as dangerous outsider is that Clay is not entirely alien in his yearnings. Chiori Miyagawa probes the blue fire in all of us that burns just beneath the surface. The ramifications of aggression only become clear in acts of violence that cannot be undone but are certain to be repeated. In moments of self-reflection or outbursts of frustration, each of the characters clamors for a life beyond the borders of decency. Amy, Clays's rebellious younger sister, expresses a sensibility that she believes she shares with her brother: "the thing that eats your insides slowly, so slowly that you don't even notice until the hole is so big your entire being can crumple into it." As she vacillates between loyalty to her brother and compassion for her parents, her memories of fears, disappointments, and guilt cause her to question her place in the cosmic order: "Where do I fit in, this cycle of births, monsters, and angels? In this dense bright, my hands do not deserve to touch the clear sea. But then where shall I wash off my red? How can I go home?" In order to support Clay, she feigns pregnancy to obtain money from her parents for an abortion, and she only turns away from him when she can no longer bear his brutality.

Even those who find pleasure in the sanctity of home and the comfort of routine must discipline the urge to escape with punishing images of bodily harm or dissolution. Clay's dutiful brother Timothy confesses: "I scoop a handful of sharp jagged crystal pieces from my dream, and scatter them on my bed on the nights I can't sleep because I'm choking on the ashes of my fantasies." And although the young wife Anne imagines the "Milky Way" on her ceiling and her "left shoulder" disappearing into the "white light," she reminds herself that in the "fabric of history, my blood is water. So I should sleep." A waking sleep is the salve for what ails them, and home, though fraught with puzzling memories and "loves lost and found," becomes the resting place in this life.

With sleep, however, come dreams, the repository of memory. Miyagawa's characters hold fast to their fragile memories and mystical thinking to ward off loss and achieve a kind of immortality. Omens of death are omnipresent. In Chikamatsu's play the young wife breaks the tooth of a comb while smoothing her daughter's hair, and she fears that this signals separation. In Miyagawa's play, Clay breaks the glass in Rebecca's locket that contains the image of her grandmother. Breaking a mirror "feels like death" says Rebecca, "particularly a glass with a person inside. It makes destiny more specific." The jealous Clay will not compete with her memories. He wants to create her world only in his image. In another scene that repeats itself just before Anne's murder, her husband James accidentally shatters the glass on a framed picture of Anne. In this "breathless second of circular motion descending," James fears that he has lost everything in his life "in this galaxy of a broken likeness of my love." When the scene repeats itself, and he is overwhelmed with anxiety, James yearns to "rewind the second" so that he can regain his earlier self, before doubt sets in and he fears that "he has lived his life in distraction." In both scenes, he phones his wife Anne for reassurance, and the ring echoes unanswered in the harrowing conclusion of the play.

Miyagawa draws on fragments of cultural memory that she finds in the interstices of time. A poetic dramatist, she incorporates figures, images, and language that can be translated into "a feeling that we can all recall from somewhere in our lives, from sometime in our pasts." [3] One such figure is White Fox, Chikamatsu's Mountain Priest summoned to help Yohei's sister recover from what we soon realize is a feigned malady to protect her brother's claim on the household. Miyagawa's White Fox appears not only as the messenger of the great Buddha Amitaba, enabling the believer to be reborn in paradise, but also, as he tells Amy, a "listener, a healer, a prophet, a sympathizer of your eclipsing soul." He answers to many needs. Some might see him as a cult leader; others a psychoanalyst. He discerns that Amy's phantom child is her childhood infatuation with Clay, the "magic" that she believed was true until the winter light revealed it as "nothing but twigs." Still, Clay inhabits her, and White Fox cannot fathom the reason for Clay's "soul raging and homeless."

Interspersed with the language of realism that propels the action are the poetic reveries of characters that move in and out of temporal and spatial dimensions. Amy recalls Clay's penchant for "Superman comic books, painted cloth Koinobori in May for the Boys' Day, and white tree barks meant to be burned to guide the ancestor's spirits during Obon in August."

Rebecca longs for a silk kimono with a sash on a high waist like the courtesans of Tennoji House. In a dream-like moment, Rebecca and Clay enact a fantasy that alludes to the poetic travel scene (*michiyuki*) between the doomed lovers intended to transform their final journey into a lyrical movement toward rebirth. On New Year's Eve, Rebecca suggests that at midnight they cab on the Manhattan Bridge, see the Brooklyn Bridge and the "man-made stars…bridging fierce needs across dull water…."

Miyagawa, of course, creates an entirely new play from this Bunraku source, and develops the story through the dialogues and monologues of her characters rather than a chanter (*tayu*) who sings or speaks the dialogue as well as narrative passages. Still, her language resonates with the shifts in lyrical and dramatic voices found in joruri chanting. Chikamatsu's collaborator, the chanter Gidayu, described joruri as a stream with "rapids and quiet pools." [4] The rapids refer to the dramatic moments in which dialogue and action move quickly; the deep pools refer to the songs of lyrical depth and power that establish mood and theme. Chiori Miyagawa's stylistic innovations evoke the metaphor of "rapids and pools"; through music, movement, and poetic language, she establishes an ominous and urgent tone lurking just beyond the yearnings for love and transcendence expressed in the lyrical reflections of her characters.

The title of the play—*Woman Killer*—alerts the viewer to impending violence, and there can be no doubt that gender is central to the act of aggression. Clay's violent dance in the shadows precedes scenes in which he stalks, corners, and threatens the women in his life, and presages the murder. Clay is not simply Anne's killer; he is a woman killer. He murders one woman to possess another, and when he takes a knife to his victim, he slays a body associated with the saintly family that he abhors. As he slips and slides in Anne's blood, he prays to God to promise her life everlasting. Clay knows that he is caught in a cycle of hell, but he revels in his freedom from "home" as well as "sanity." His "luck in this world" is just beginning.

Sharon Friedman,
The Gallatin School, New York University

ENDNOTES
[1] Tsubouchi Shoyo qtd. in William Lee, "Chikamatsu and Dramatic Literature in the Meiji Period," in *Inventing the Classics: Modernity, National Identity, and Japanese Literature*, eds. Haruo Shirane and Tomi Suzuki (Stanford: Stanford University Press, 2000) 190.

[2] Haruo Shirane, ed., *Early Modern Japanese Literature: An Anthology, 1600-1900* (New York: Columbia University Press, 2002) 236.

[3] Chiori Miyagawa, " Do Poets Keep Secrets?" www.drunkenboat.com/db9/poetics_essays/miyagawa/poetics_miy a.html.

[4] Takemoto Gidayu qtd. in Shirane, 241.

WOMAN KILLER

by Chiori Miyagawa

(actors: Kristin DiSpaltro, Crispin Freeman)
Photo credit: Sonoko Kawahara

Characters

CLAY, a man in his mid-20s

REBECCA, Clay's girlfriend

TIMOTHY, Clay's younger brother, 20

AMY, Clay's younger sister, 17

MOTHER (ELIZABETH), Clay's mother

FATHER (HENRY), Clay's father

ANNE, a woman in her 30s

JAMES, Anne's husband

WHITE FOX, a mountain priest

MICHAEL

JOE

Co-Worker

Time: 2001

Place: Brooklyn, NY

Woman Killer was produced by Crossing Jamaica Avenue and HERE Arts Center and directed by Sonoko Kawahara. It opened on September 6, 2001, in downtown New York City, five days before 9.11. I am grateful to Martin Denton and The New York Theatre Experience, Inc. for first publishing the play in *Plays and Playwrights 2002* and saving it from the ashes of a broken heart. I am grateful to everyone who came to see the play after we managed to reopen it one week later, in the neighborhood where we could still see and smell the smoke. Thank you to Ron Cohen for keeping the cast together. Thank you to all the cast members, who performed this play about violence in a violent time.

Chiori Miyagawa

CAST:

Clay….……………………......Crispin Freeman

Anne….…...………………………......Hope Salas

Rebecca……………………Kristine DiSpaltro

Mother….…...………………....Connie Edgerly

Timothy………….….…………Michael Braun

Amy………………………………...Kei Arita

Father…………………………..Ronald Cohen

James…………………………….Shawn Randall

White Fox, Michael, Joe, Co-Worker
…………………………………....…..Paul H. Juhn

NOTES:

"Some Years From Now" Lyrics © 2001 by Mark
Campbell. Printed with the permission of the
lyricist.

Original music for the song may be ordered by
contacting Dan Sonenberg at:
dsonenberg@maine.rr.com

Woman Killer is inspired by 1728 Japanese Bunraku
Puppet play, *The Woman Killer and the Hell of Oil*,
by Chikamatsu Monzaemon.

The format editor for this book is Lori Fromowitz.

SCENE 1

Lights up on ANNE. Singing.

Some Years From Now

When we're in our golden years
Some years from now
Our lives will not be so complex
We can up and get away
Or stay in and read all day
Maybe even rediscover sex.

Looking at our golden years
Some years from now
The day-to-day will be a breeze.
Though the children will be grown,
They'll have children of their own
We can spoil as rotten as we please.

Until then
There are mouths to be fed,
And shoes to be tied,
And beds to be made.
Until then
There are skirts to be hemmed,
And tests to be passed,
And boys to fend off.

Until then
There are a million wrongs to make right,
And a million kisses good night.

It will be our golden years
Some years from now
Although it's hard to say just when.
But imagine how sublime
When we look back at this time
Some years from now
And laugh at how
Serious we used to be—back then.

Lights down. ANNE disappears.

Music, violent. Lights up. CLAY's dance in shadows, violent.

Music cuts off. CLAY becomes still. A light on his face.

CLAY: But how can I go home? How can I get off this train and walk toward the beginning, when it never began in the first place, and where is this first place, and what is *it* that never began?

Black.
Lights up on CLAY and his girlfriend REBECCA.
Dream scene. Threatening.

REBECCA: What do you want?

CLAY: Nothing.

CLAY advances on REBECCA menacingly.
REBECCA senses danger.

REBECCA: Stay there.

CLAY: Why are you scared?

They circle each other.

REBECCA: Clay, it's me.

CLAY: I know who you are.

REBECCA: Go home.

CLAY: I can't.

They stare at each other. Tense.

Black.

SCENE 2

Halloween. Lights up on Anne's apartment. ANNE is
putting away children's costumes.

The doorbell rings.

CLAY: Trick or treat!

ANNE: Clay! Come in.

CLAY enters. He is wearing a large pair of feather wings of mixed odd colors.

CLAY: I was on my way to a party and thought I'd drop by and see you. Where is James?

ANNE: He's still at work. What kind of a bird are you?

CLAY: I'm not a bird.

ANNE: The wings.

CLAY: I'm an angel.

ANNE: *(teasing)* I don't know if it's the right costume for you.

CLAY: What should I be instead?

ANNE: Devil?

CLAY: There is no irony in that.

ANNE: I suppose. Did you make the win yourself?

CLAY: Bought them white. I added the colors.

ANNE: I don't seem to have the time or desire to do those things for myself anymore. I have to do them for my children now. It's like I'm reliving parts of my life over through them. Only now I'm watching, walking parallel to the actual path of life's discoveries.

CLAY: Is that strange?

ANNE: Sometimes. Sometimes even sad. But most of the time delightful.

CLAY: Hey, do you want to go to this party with me?

ANNE: What am I going to do with my kids?

CLAY: Bring them.

ANNE: Don't be silly.

CLAY: *(half serious)* It's the night of the devil. The only night that you can be something other than yourself. Without consequence or punishment. Shed your fears, Anne. Sacrifice your children. Abandon your beliefs. Bite the candied apple. Come with me.

ANNE: *(laughs)* We already had our spooky Halloween outing. Would you like some chocolate?

CLAY: We used to party. James too.

ANNE: Yes. We used to. When we were carefree and privileged.

CLAY: We are still.

ANNE: Not carefree. I have a lot to care for. James. The kids.

CLAY: It's boring.

ANNE: Some of us grow up.

CLAY: You deserve a medal for growing up.

CLAY plucks a fake feather from one of his wings and goes up close to ANNE. He threads the feather through a buttonhole on her shirt. He then holds her wrist and examines her bracelet.

CLAY: Very nice. A gift from James?

ANNE: For our tenth anniversary.

CLAY: Diamonds and gold. It sparkles on you.

During this JAMES enters. He stops and looks at them silently until ANNE looks up and sees him.

ANNE: *(with joy)* James.

ANNE goes to kiss JAMES as CLAY turns around to see him.

CLAY: Hey, buddy.

JAMES: Clay. Didn't recognize you with your wings.

CLAY: A costume party.

JAMES: What are you doing here?

CLAY: Came by to see if you wanted to go with me.

JAMES: Me? Or Anne?

CLAY: You. Both.

JAMES: We can't get a sitter with such a short notice, you know that. Especially on Halloween.

CLAY: Right.

ANNE: Don't you have a date, Clay?

CLAY: I don't want the bother.

ANNE: I'm sure there are many women who would be happy to be your angel mate for the night. Carefree and privileged.

CLAY: Not really. Anyway, I should get going. Out to the haunted city!

He kisses ANNE, shakes JAMES' hand and exits.

Pause.

ANNE: Are you hungry?

JAMES: Yeah.

ANNE: Hamburger ok?

JAMES: I'm tired of hamburgers. Can't we have a little more imagination?

ANNE: We?

JAMES: Ok. You. If you didn't spend all afternoon yakking with Clay, I wouldn't have to live with hamburgers again.

ANNE: The girls and I were out trick or treating this afternoon. Clay was only here for ten minutes before you came home. Besides, you like hamburgers. And we don't have it that often.

JAMES: Did you know he was coming over?

ANNE: James. What are you asking?

JAMES: Nothing.

ANNE: Clay lives five minutes away. He comes over all the time without notice.

JAMES: Not so much anymore.

ANNE: Did you have a bad day?

JAMES: I've been hearing things about Clay.

ANNE: What things?

JAMES: He got into a fight at a bar about a month ago. Injured someone with a broken beer bottle. His parents took out their checkbook to fix the situation.

ANNE: This isn't the first time they had to pay Clay's way out of trouble.

JAMES: The fight was over a girl. Someone who works as an escort or something.

ANNE: Where did you hear all this?

JAMES: I ran into Clay's uncle. He has a hard time trying to keep Clay out of trouble at the job too.

ANNE: Clay has always been restless.

Pause.

JAMES: Did you want to go to the party with him?

ANNE: No.

Pause.

ANNE: How about some pasta?

JAMES: Sounds good.

ANNE turns to go to the kitchen.

JAMES: Anne?

ANNE: Yes?

JAMES: Did you miss me today?

ANNE: More than usual?

JAMES: I don't know.

ANNE: You go to work every day.

JAMES: Right. Every day.

ANNE: I miss you every day.

JAMES: Today more than yesterday?

ANNE: What's wrong?

JAMES: Time passes between us.

ANNE: Time passes with us, James.

JAMES: I'm hungry.

SCENE 3

REBECCA and CLAY in bed.

CLAY takes off a locket from REBECCA 's neck. He fumbles when he attempts to open it and drops the locket.

Pause. They both look at the locket on the floor. REBECCA picks it up and opens it.

REBECCA: The glass is broken.

CLAY: I'll buy you another one.

REBECCA: It was my grandmother's.

CLAY: I just wanted to see what she looked like.

REBECCA: I think it's bad luck. It feels like death.

CLAY: No, Rebecca. Breaking a mirror is bad luck.

REBECCA: It's glass with an image of a person inside. It just makes destiny more specific.

CLAY: It's not destiny. Just a superstition. Besides, your grandmother is already dead. Nothing else is going to happen to her.

Pause.

CLAY: I'll make it up to you. For the loss of your grandmother.

REBECCA: I want a silver locket from Tiffany's.

CLAY: Anything you want.

REBECCA: Two. An oval one and a heart shaped one. I saw them in a catalogue.

CLAY: Anything you want.

REBECCA: Anything?

CLAY: I love you.

REBECCA: You broke my locket on purpose. Because I liked it. Because I wore it every day. It touched my flesh more than you did.

CLAY: Strange thing to say, Rebecca.

REBECCA: I know you.

CLAY: If you had to choose between the memories of your grandmother and a future with me, which would you choose?

REBECCA: I can't choose between something I already have and something that's yet to exist.

CLAY: I exist. She doesn't.

REBECCA: Why are you jealous of my memories?

CLAY: I don't want you to look away.

REBECCA: We all live with memories.

CLAY: I want you to look at me. Always.

SCENE 4

Thanksgiving dinner. Clay's parents' house.

MOTHER: Timothy made the cranberry sauce.

TIMOTHY: From scratch.

ANNE: It's delicious. I'm impressed.

TIMOTHY: I went to the farmer's market for fresh cranberries.

ANNE: And what did you contribute to this Thanksgiving dinner, Amy?

AMY: I watched.

MOTHER: I made her help me with everything. When she gets married, she will have to do all this herself. She should start learning it now.

AMY: I'll pick everything up at Balducci's. Including the cranberry sauce.

TIMOTHY: Don't you like my cranberry sauce?

AMY: I do. But it's too wholesome and good for when I have to become a house-wife. I need a little bitterness.

ANNE: Being a housewife can be sweet, Amy.

JAMES: How's college treating you, Timothy?

TIMOTHY: Good. I'm playing soccer this year.

FATHER: His grades are excellent. He is thinking about going to law school.

TIMOTHY: Dad, I don't know about that yet.

MOTHER: Clay just had an interview for a new job.

CLAY: It's nothing, really.

JAMES: You didn't tell me about this.

CLAY: Because it's not a big deal, James. I'm just looking for something that pays better.

FATHER: I will pay you more if you show me that you're serious about our family business.

CLAY: We've been through this before.

FATHER: You have to earn money, just like trust.

MOTHER: Henry. You can't keep him forever. He has to be on his own eventually.

FATHER: I'd like him to be by my side.

CLAY: *(to ANNE, indicating that this conversation is over)* I have to miss your pumpkin pie this year. I have to go now.

ANNE: Where are you going?

CLAY: I'm having dessert with my girlfriend's family.

Awkward pause. Clay's parents are tense.

ANNE: I'd like to meet your girlfriend sometime.

What's her name?

CLAY: Rebecca.

ANNE: I'm sorry she couldn't be here today.

CLAY: Me too. I'm also sorry that you didn't bring your kids. Where are they?

ANNE: They are with my parents in Oregon. They wanted to go on an adventure on their own. So I put them on the plane and sent them off.

JAMES: It was very brave of her.

ANNE: It was brave of our girls. They are only six and eight. I didn't get on the plane and leave home until I was twenty.

JAMES: It was very brave of you.

CLAY: I agree. You are a good mother, Anne.

ANNE: Thank you, Clay.

SCENE 5

Late at night, the same day.

AMY: You didn't really go to Rebecca's for dessert, did you?

CLAY: If you go into Manhattan, you can always find a bar that's open, even on the day of the judgment.

TIMOTHY: Why do you need to do that? You know it upsets Mom every time you leave a family gathering in the middle.

CLAY: I couldn't sit there for one more minute. I don't have the enormous capacity for bullshiting that you have, Timothy.

TIMOTHY: It's called being decent.

CLAY: All those decent people around the table being decent to each other makes me want to puke. Every Thanksgiving we do the same thing, eat the same food, and have the same people over for the same conversation.

TIMOTHY: Don't you like Anne and James?

AMY: I can't imagine how Anne stands being at home all the time. Cooking and cleaning. I thought women stopped doing those things for men.

TIMOTHY: You know she has two daughters. And she and James are very much in love.

AMY: I think she likes Clay.

TIMOTHY: That's insane. We've known her since her family moved into the neighbor- hood when she was in high school.

CLAY: It's really too bad she went and had a slew of kids. She's still young and attractive.

AMY: A model house wife. A picture of domestic simplicity. It's very boring.

TIMOTHY: You are jealous of her.

AMY: Now who is insane?

CLAY: Anne is pretty to look at, but I don't think there is any passion left in her.

TIMOTHY: Tell me what you think passion is.

CLAY: Something you wouldn't know, Timothy.

TIMOTHY: I don't think you know me well enough to say that.

CLAY: When have you known passion? Tell me one incident when you felt passion.

Pause.

AMY: It's not necessary.

TIMOTHY: You have no idea.

CLAY: Tell us.

TIMOTHY: I scoop a handful of sharp jagged crystal pieces from my dream, and scatter them on my bed on the nights I can't sleep because I'm choking on the ashes of my fantasies. You are wrong if you think it's easy to get it right, to be a good student, to look good, to respect women, to save money, to plan for the future. You are wrong if you think these are the things I really want in life.

CLAY: What do you want then?

TIMOTHY: I try not to want. I spend all my passion trying not to want the wrong things.

Pause.

CLAY: You're mixing up boredom and passion.

TIMOTHY: You've been mixing up harm and passion all your life.

CLAY: Yeah. I want so much, want so much, I can hardly stand it. It's blue, sharp clear icy blue, and so scorching hot it burns my eyes. Blue fire. I am so thirsty I can taste my own death.

Pause.

TIMOTHY: Clay. Passion will kill you in the end.

Long pause.

AMY: Anne is very pretty. And a good person. I like her. Really.

SCENE 6

A few days later. MOTHER is holding a credit card statement. She shows it to CLAY.
TIMOTHY comes in during their argument.

MOTHER: Would you explain this to me?

CLAY: It's a cash advance for one thousand.

MOTHER: I did not give you permission for this.

CLAY: I'm tired of discussing money.

MOTHER: We're not discussing money. We're discussing your stealing.

CLAY: I'm tried of that too.

MOTHER: What did you do with the money?

CLAY: Sounds like we're discussing money to me.

MOTHER: Are you in trouble?

CLAY: No, Mom. Don't worry.

MOTHER: Don't mock me. You owe me an explanation.

TIMOTHY: Answer her, Clay.

CLAY: I don't have an answer. You're the one with all the answers, Timothy.

TIMOTHY: Was it for drugs?

CLAY: You think you're smart, don't you?

TIMOTHY: It wouldn't be the first time.

MOTHER: If you get caught again with drug possession, you will go to jail this time.

CLAY: I'll try not to get caught.

MOTHER: Clay, tell me the truth!

CLAY: It's not that serious. I rented a limo and went out with Rebecca. I'm sorry, but you know all my credit cards are maxed out, and it was her birthday. I had no other choice.

TIMOTHY: That is absurd. You could have just stayed home.

CLAY: No. I couldn't have.

TIMOTHY: No mater how much you want it, how much you think you need it, at any given moment of your life, something will be out of your reach. You have to live with that like the rest of us.

CLAY: Not me.

MOTHER: Why does Rebecca have to go out in a limousine? Doesn't she know you can't afford it?

CLAY: But you can afford it.

MOTHER: That is not the point.

CLAY: Mom, I'll pay you back. I promise. Okay?

He kisses MOTHER's cheek.

CLAY: I'm sorry. But no one got hurt. And Rebecca and I had a really good time. Don't stay angry with me. I won't do it again.

MOTHER: Be careful with someone who asks for more than you can give. In materials or emotions.

CLAY: There is no need to worry.

CLAY exits.

TIMOTHY: Are you going to let him just walk away again?

MOTHER: I'm tired, Timothy. I don't have in me to discipline him anymore.

TIMOTHY: You're not helping him by always covering for him. Let him grow up, for god's sake.

MOTHER: He is grown up already. Sometimes I wish he would just go away. He has worn me out.

Pause.

MOTHER: I'm glad you are home.

TIMOTHY: You know I'm going skiing over Christmas. Are you going to be okay without me?

SCENE 7

Music, violent. CLAY's dance in the shadows, violent. Music cuts off abruptly. CLAY becomes still. Lights up on Amy's room.

Three weeks later.

CLAY: You have to help me.

AMY: Why are you so stupid to borrow money from somebody like Joe?

CLAY: Because I have no money. I haven't been paying my credit card bills. The collection agency is after me. I'll have to declare bankruptcy pretty soon.

AMY: If Joe doesn't get his money back, he will kill you.

CLAY: He won't. But he'll hurt me. Embarrass me.

AMY: Explain it to Mom and Dad. They'll cover it for you, I'm sure.

CLAY: You want me to tell them I owe a drug dealer sixteen thousand dollars?

AMY: You said it wasn't for drugs.

CLAY: Not all of it.

AMY: It's Rebecca, isn't it? What did you buy her? What did she ask for?

CLAY: Everything she deserves.

AMY: Clay, Rebecca is dangerous for you. She has no limits to her desire. She will devour your longing, your illusions, your sex and your money. The empty space in her is bigger than you. You'll disappear in her.

CLAY: That's what I want.

AMY: She's not worth giving up the chance for normal life that Timothy talks about. She's only a whore.

CLAY: Shut the hell up!

AMY: You know she is. If you don't, tell me she isn't a whore!

CLAY goes for AMY. He grabs her neck. AMY gasps. He slowly releases her but keeps his hand on her. He changes his energy form violent to sexual.

CLAY: Do you remember when we were kids, we went back every day to the school ground after everyone had gone home, and played until the sun was dead and the air was dusky?

AMY: Some days, the sky would go orange before turning grey. Hours after that, I still had orange in my throat.

CLAY: One time there was a big hole in the ground. I think they were in the process of putting in new swings. The workers had left for the evening.

AMY: I remember.

CLAY: I hopped into the hole, made you stand still on the edge of it, and threw a stone at you.

AMY: It hit me.

CLAY: I didn't think I could really hit you. I was looking up at you from the bottom of the hole. You were a silhouette against the faint faint orange.

AMY: You hit me. I cried. You promised to tell Mom and Dad that you fell. When we got home, Mom flipped out seeing blood on your forehead. As soon as she asked what happened, you said,

AMY: Clay hit me with a stone.

CLAY: I hated you.

AMY: I was just a little girl then.

CLAY: You have to help me. You're my sister.

AMY: Only half. Only the half that longs for darkness, for the shadows of the unattainable.

CLAY: You know I love you.

AMY: What makes you think they'll give me the money?

CLAY: Because you're the baby of the family. And Dad is your real father.

AMY: He's your father too. We are a family.

CLAY: I've asked for money too many times already. Do this for me. Sixteen thousand dollars. Get it for me.

CLAY kisses AMY on the lips tenderly.

SCENE 8

A few days later. The house is decorated with Christmas ornaments.

AMY: Talk to Dad for me.

MOTHER: Are you sure that's what you want to do?

AMY: What else do you think I should do, Mom?

MOTHER: I want us to be sure that we want to bring your father into this.

AMY: I don't think we can hide it from him, Mom.

MOTHER: Why do you want him to know? He has enough worries.

AMY: This should be one of them.

MOTHER: Who is the father?

AMY: It doesn't matter.

MOTHER: It matters.   You did this with another person. It matters.

AMY: There is no father because there isn't going to be a baby. I just need the money.

MOTHER: We'll go see the doctor together.

AMY: No. I want to do this alone. Please just give me the money.

MOTHER: I want you to be safe.

AMY: Please just give me the money or you'll ruin me.

MOTHER: What do you need?

AMY: Sixteen thousand dollars.

MOTHER: You're not making any sense.

AMY: It's not just for an abortion. I need certain things.

MOTHER: What things?

AMY: I need a bridge, protection, sharpness and silence, sixteen thousand dollars.

MOTHER: Amy?

AMY: I'm carrying a devil child. If I don't do this right, I will be damaged forever. I'll never be able to cook a Thanksgiving turkey. Do you really want to risk that, Mom? What is life for without a turkey? Huh?

MOTHER: Amy, please.

AMY: I'm pregnant with everything that was ever wrong with this family, Mom. It was inevitable. The only way out of doom is money. You agree, don't you?

MOTHER: Calm down, Amy.

AMY: You and Dad fix the world with your checkbooks, don't you? You send money to cancer research, to children of the third world, to the animal rights people, and to the relief efforts for the disaster in Indonesia. For years you wrote checks to keep Clay out of juvenile halls and to keep Timothy in private schools. You can write a check for me for once to save me from becoming the devil's concubine, can't you?

MOTHER: Don't be ridiculous. Let's concentrate on how we can get help for you.

AMY: Yes! Let's concentrate! I need a cow and a needle and a noodle and toilet paper by the truckloads. I need sixteen thousand francs, freaks. (screams) Ahhhh. I'm in pain. Mom! Mom! Where are you?

MOTHER: I'm right here. Henry!

AMY: I'm dying.

MOTHER: Henry!

FATHER rushes in.

FATHER: What's the matter?

MOTHER: Amy is sick. Call an ambulance.

AMY: No! You take me to the hospital, I'll kill myself. You know what I need. Save me, Dad.

He holds AMY.

FATHER: Shhh. It's all right. Whatever it is, I'll take care of it. Don't worry.

AMY: Punctured, burned, scraped, frozen. We are in the ice age and dinosaurs are extinct. The miracle of greatness is vanished, but I'll stain this planet with my blood before it's all over.

I'll kill myself. I'll kill myself. I'LL KILL MYSELF! MERRY CHRISTMAS!

SCENE 9

The winter streets. CLAY and JAMES run into each other.

JAMES: How have you been, buddy? You don't come around much anymore.

CLAY: I'm sorry about that, James. I've been busy. How's your family?

JAMES: Good. I think we are going to buy a house in Brooklyn Heights. We looked at one over the weekend.

CLAY: Are you going to move away from the neighborhood?

JAMES: It's not that far.

CLAY: Brooklyn Heights. That's nice. Nicer than this damn place.

JAMES: What're you talking about? This is the crossroads of Brooklyn: southeast to Nagasaki, northeast to Kyoto, Southwest to Manhattan, northeast to the Temple Kanzeon. It's a great place. Just look at the Grand Army Plaza.

CLAY: *(forcing an air of sincerity)* A house in the Heights is better. I envy you. You've got it made. A good job, nice wife, kids. That's what life is all about.

JAMES: Bullshit. You don't envy me. I think you like your own life quite a bit.

CLAY: *(exaggerated)* You're wrong. I'm miserable.

JAMES: *(teasing)* You've got your tough friends to hang out and go drinking with. You have a sexy little girlfriend I hear. You really want to give that all up to be a responsible family man?

CLAY: Sure. Anytime.

JAMES: You're funny.

CLAY: Aren't you happy with your life?

JAMES: I am. I just know too much.

CLAY: I don't know enough.

JAMES: I guess that's the difference.

CLAY: When I was a kid, the future was a blank sheet of paper. Wait. No. I didn't even know the paper existed. I wasn't aware of the vast whiteness in front me.

JAMES: I guess we become adults when we begin to see that paper.

CLAY: Filling in the space is tedious. We can still end up with nothing in the end.

JAMES: Not nothing.

CLAY: What?

JAMES: Not nothing. Family. Loves lost and found. Images. Memories. Not nothing, Clay.

CLAY: Whatever. I'd rather be free.

JAMES: See? You like your life.

Pause.

CLAY: *(sincerely)* Go home James. While you still can.

JAMES: I will. Come over sometime soon. We'll watch the game. Drink some beers. Like before.

CLAY: Before what?

JAMES: I don't know. Just before.

CLAY: *(with an enthusiastic air)* Sure. Sounds good. Sounds like fun. Sounds real good.

JAMES: Soon?

CLAY: *(innocent)* Yeah, I'm looking forward to it, buddy. Merry Christmas.

SCENE 10

New Year's Eve. CLAY waits for REBECCA in front of a nightclub. She enters with a man.

CLAY: What's up, Rebecca.

REBECCA: Clay. What are you doing here?

CLAY: I heard a rumor that you'd be at this club with this asshole, instead of at your sister's like you told me.

MICHAEL: Excuse me?

CLAY: I wasn't talking to you.

REBECCA: It didn't work out with my sister tonight.

CLAY: I thought it was a family tradition that you two spend New Year's Eve together.

REBECCA: It is. It just didn't work out this year.

CLAY: Why didn't you call me?

REBECCA: I didn't know how to find you.

CLAY: You knew how to find him.

MICHAEL: Rebecca and I have plans for the evening.

CLAY: You're crazy if you think you're going in to that club with her.

REBECCA: Baby, I'm sorry for the misunderstanding.

CLAY: Misunderstanding?

REBECCA: I'm here. You found me. I'm yours and yours alone.

REBECCA moves close to CLAY.

MICHAEL: Jesus.

CLAY: Get lost.

MICHAEL: Rebecca, why don't you tell him that two hours ago you said you were mine? Mine alone?

REBECCA: It was a dream, Michael.

MICHAEL: Slut.

CLAY jumps MICHAEL. They fight. REBECCA watches.

MICHAEL: I'm not coming back. Do you understand me, Rebecca? This is the last time!

MICHAEL exits.

CLAY: There goes your rich boyfriend.

REBECCA: I missed you.

Pause.

REBECCA: Hold me. I'm cold.

CLAY does so.

CLAY: That's a nice dress. Did he buy it for you?

REBECCA: No. I put it on my Amex. Didn't you promise me a dress for New Year?

CLAY: When I thought you were coming out with me tonight.

REBECCA: Here I am.

CLAY: What do you want from me?

REBECCA: A silk kimono in red chrysanthemum patterns that I can wear with a sash on high waist like the courtesans of Tennonji House.

CLAY: Tennonji House?

REBECCA: Come on, I know you've been there. On 42nd Street off the Tokaido path.

CLAY: Silk kimonos are expensive.

REBECCA: I thought you said anything I wanted. I only want it for you anyway.

CLAY: What are we doing, Rebecca?

REBECCA: Can't we just hang out without promises or analysis? It's boring. You know you're special to me. We're like Siamese twins of the soul. No one can cut us apart.

CLAY kisses REBECCA passionately.

REBECCA: It will be midnight soon. Do you want to go see the Brooklyn Bridge?

CLAY: If you want.

REBECCA: We can take a cab on the Manhattan Bridge and see the Brooklyn Bridge from there. Man-made stars sparkling, bridging fierce needs across dull water, against the skyline of greatness. Then we can drive up Fifth Avenue. Did you see the Empire State Building tonight? It's blue.

CLAY: Deep blue.

REBECCA: Touch my lips, Clay.

CLAY: Why?

REBECCA: You open doors in me when you kiss me.

CLAY: Where do the doors lead to?

REBECCA: Places I've never been before. New places. Where my ghosts live.

CLAY: Ghosts?

REBECCA: Deep, disengaging my heart from years of wanting.

CLAY: I'm honored.

REBECCA: Fuck you.

CLAY: Don't leave me.

REBECCA: Why are you scared?

CLAY: I'm stepping around quicksand. At any time I can slip and fall into it.

REBECCA: What would happen if you fall in?

CLAY: I don't know. Rebecca , if you betray me, I will kill you.

REBECCA: Whatever is waiting for you in the quicksand has nothing to do with me.

CLAY: Doesn't matter. I'll kill you anyway.

REBECCA: I don't care. None of this is real anyway. I can give it up anytime.

CLAY: I doubt you'll be saying that when I have a knife against your throat.

REBECCA: You hate me, don't you?

CLAY: I love you. I will kill you.

SCENE 11

The next day. TIMOTHY enters the house with bags.

FATHER: Timothy! I didn't know you were coming home for New Years.

TIMOTHY: Mom called me about Amy.

FATHER: She shouldn't have bothered you. Amy is going to be fine.

TIMOTHY: Where is she?

FATHER: She is in her room. Don't worry.

TIMOTHY: I also got a call from Uncle David. He thinks Clay is trying to embezzle money from the company.

FATHER: Why didn't David tell me this?

TIMOTHY: He didn't want to upset you. He wanted me to talk to Clay. But I thought you should know. Dad, you need to make some decisions about Clay.

FATHER: Deep in my heart, I knew I could not trust him.

TIMOTHY: Fire him. Throw him out of the house. You have been too lenient and forgiving with him, with both of us. When we were small, the only one who got punished for mischief was Amy. I know she is your blood child. But you're Clay's and my father too. We have had no other.

FATHER: Your father was my best friend. Clay looks so much like him now. Sometimes I have to stop myself from calling him Walter. Sometimes I'm back in time, before the accident that killed him, before the sorrow that buried me, and I see Walter. I want to say, where have you been, Walter? We are both young and strong again. I reach over to grab his shoulder, and just that moment, I realize it's Clay.

TIMOTHY: All my life I have covered for him, cleaned up after him, and apologized for him. I'm sick of it. You've spoiled him rotten with the best stereo, the best bicycle, and the best clothes. Made him rotten.

FATHER: I've given you the same.

TIMOTHY: But I'm grateful.

FATHER: I know.

TIMOTHY: He hurts you. I don't.

FATHER: You are good.

TIMOTHY: Mom wants you to be firmer with Clay. She thinks you're hesitant because you're his stepfather. Dad, Clay has tortured her soul. How many times has she told us that she doesn't care if he were gone from our lives forever?

FATHER: Your mother loves Clay.

TIMOTHY: She says she has no love left for him.

FATHER: Do you believe her?

TIMOTHY: I do.

Pause.

TIMOTHY: I want to believe her. His drinking, fighting, lying, dreaming of damage, taking souls, trampling, polluting, turning, cracked, broken, no way back, and his shame, his shame should make her stop loving him. But despite all that, I know she still loves him best. Still loves *him* best.

SCENE 12

The same place as scene 1. They circle each other. CLAY is threatening. Dream scene.

AMY: What do you want?

CLAY: Nothing.

AMY: Stay there.

CLAY: Why are you scared?

AMY: Go home.

CLAY: I can't.

AMY: You can. You can still go home.

CLAY: After a certain point, there is no way back home. Home is a lie anyway. Life, is a big lie. This stupidity, this resignation, two cars parked on the drive way, barbecues and beaches and funerals, meaningless, deprived, boring.

AMY: Clay, it's me.

CLAY: No one is true. You are not me, and I don't know you.

AMY: I know *you*. It's a new year, Clay.

CLAY: Happy New Year! Another happy lying year!

They stare at each other. Black.

SCENE 13

JAMES is in his office. He picks up the phone and dials. It rings. ANNE picks up on the other end.

JAMES: Anne.

ANNE: Yes, honey.

JAMES: I'll be late. Have dinner without me.

ANNE: Again?

JAMES: I have to catch up with work. I'm behind because of the holidays.

ANNE: Other people have holidays too.

JAMES: I have a lot to do.

ANNE: Always.

JAMES: I'll see you later.

ANNE: James?

JAMES: What?

ANNE: Would you like dinner when you get home?

JAMES: No. I'll just grab a hamburger on the way home.

ANNE: It's no trouble. I was creative today. I made roasted potato and fennel soup and poached salmon.

JAMES: Sounds good. But you don't have to wait for me.

ANNE: I'll wait for you.

JAMES: All right. See you later.

ANNE: James?

JAMES: What?

ANNE: Did you miss me today?

JAMES: More than usual?

ANNE: I don't know.

JAMES: I go to work every day.

ANNE: Right. Every day.

JAMES: I have to go.

ANNE: See you soon.

Click. Dial tone.

SCENE 14

Music, violent. CLAY's dance in the shadows, violent.
CLAY becomes still. A light on his face.

CLAY: We sneak into my father's company
building one o'clock in the morning and fuck on
the floor of his office. Rebecca is menstruating;
she drips dark blood mixed with milky seamen on
his plushy beige carpet. This is how it feels to live.
My hands are covered with her blood. We
baptize each other in the liquid of the mystery
from which all human cravings arise.

*Lights up on REBECCA, half dressed, lying on the
floor.*

CLAY: Let's go.

REBECCA: Can't we just sleep here a little?

CLAY: We can't stay here. When the sun comes
up, our love making will become a crime.

REBECCA: That's what you wanted.

CLAY: You're wrong.

REBECCA: You have something raging and homeless in you.

CLAY: I recognize the same in you.

REBECCA: Not me.

CLAY: The first time we met at a party, I said I liked your rhinestone earrings. You looked at me, took them off, and threw them in the trash. You didn't say a word to me.

Pause.

REBECCA: I don't want to look like a fake, even if I am.

CLAY: Go home, Rebecca. Your parents must be worried.

REBECCA: I doubt it. They don't ask themselves questions like "It's five a.m. in the morning. Do you know where your kids are?"

REBECCA gets up and gets dressed. Her beeper goes off. She checks it.

CLAY: Who is beeping you at five in the morning?

REBECCA: Wrong number.

CLAY: Don't lie to me.

REBECCA: I'm going home.

CLAY: Tell me who it was.

REBECCA: Clay, who the hell are you? What claim do you have on me?

CLAY: I love you.

REBECCA: But you don't have a place of your own and you don't have any money. All you got is a soul raging and homeless. When I get home, my knees bruised, my back carpet burned, and step into a bath with dried blood caked on my inner thighs, where will your heart be, Clay? Will you be making plans for living happily ever after with me somewhere where there are white picket fences?

CLAY: You can't possibly dream about something so tame.

REBECCA: I want to. But not with you. Away from you.

CLAY: That will never happen.

REBECCA: We are flying without a safety net. We can crash at any time. Then what?

CLAY: You love the thrill.

REBECCA: Not always. I haven't given up on the other thing. Someday, I'm going to be a different person. I'm going to achieve a normal life.

CLAY: Why don't you leave me then?

REBECCA: I'm trying.

Pause.

REBECCA: What do *you* dream about?

CLAY: I dream about not here, not now, not me, not this. Nothing. I can't.

REBECCA: You think you're chasing me. It's you who is not mine.

CLAY: I like the smell of your blood.

Pause.

REBECCA: I love you, Clay.

SCENE 15

TIMOTHY enters Amy's room. She is in bed.

TIMOTHY: Amy, it's me.

AMY: Timothy.

TIMOTHY: What are you doing?

AMY: I'm in pain.

TIMOTHY: Did Clay put you up to this?

AMY: Are you asking me if Clay got me pregnant?

TIMOTHY: I'm asking you why you need sixteen thousand dollars.

AMY: You don't know anything.

TIMOTHY: Who does?

AMY: Me. Only me.

TIMOTHY: I don't believe you.

AMY: Life is so easy for you, Timothy.

TIMOTHY: How do you figure that?

AMY: Because you weren't born with *it*.

TIMOTHY: It?

AMY: It. That thing that eats your insides slowly, so slowly that you don't even notice until the hole is so big your entire being can crumple into it. And there you are, slipping, bleeding, cooking a turkey in the big hole until death do us part.

TIMOTHY: Us?

AMY: Me and *it*.

TIMOTHY: Why do you love Clay so much?

AMY: He has *it*. We are the same.

TIMOTHY: No, you are not. Don't go to him. Stay with me.

AMY: I don't think it's a choice. You don't understand.

TIMOTHY: How can you hurt our parents? Is he worth causing their agony? Especially Dad. He is so sad. You are his blood.

AMY: It's not all for Clay. My pain is true. They should notice it. They should notice me.

TIMOTHY: I'll stop you.

AMY: They have the money. And it's only money. It's not going to fix anything in anybody. It's only money.

TIMOTHY: It's not the money they are worried about. They don't understand your hostility. They don't understand what your demand really is.

AMY: They never have.

SCENE 16

Clay's house. The door bell rings. WHITE FOX, a mountain priest enters.

WHITE FOX: Is this the house of Henry of New York? I am the priest of fox god. I am calling at the request of the mountain brotherhood.

FATHER: I appreciate you coming, White Fox. I need your prayers for my daughter. Please wait here for a moment.

FATHER exits. CLAY enters.

CLAY: White Fox! Are you here to pray for my sister? It's a waste of time. Amy is mortally ill. No mountain priest can drive out what possesses her.

WHITE FOX: We'll see.

CLAY: What's that?

WHITE FOX: We'll see how she responds to my prayers.

CLAY: That's not satisfactory. We are paying a lot of money for your scam. I'd like to see some real exorcism, you know, her head turning and shit.

WHITE FOX: What's your name?

CLAY: Oh, no. You can't hypnotize me. I went to college. I know about these things.

WHITE FOX: What do you know?

CLAY: Do you ever speak more than one sentence at a time?

WHITE FOX: (laughs) Not when I'm with someone much wiser than me. You, for example. You are so smart and fast, you don't even breathe in between your desperate ranting to cover your guilt.

CLAY tenses up. Pause.

CLAY: You don't know anything.

WHITE FOX: Exactly my point.

CLAY: I'm not going to let you ruin me.

WHITE FOX: I'm just a simple priest who sits and meditates most of the time. I come down the mountain occasionally when I'm called upon to relieve suffering. You need not be threatened.

CLAY: Great! Why don't you relieve my suffering since you are here? And how about the people next door?

WHITE FOX: I cannot foretell the future, but I can see you are carrying a heavy burden of karma. It may defeat you if you don't dissolve it through purification.

FATHER comes back.

FATHER: She is ready for you.

CLAY: Dad. I have an urgent business to discuss with you.

FATHER: I can't deal with you right now.

CLAY: Uncle David is in trouble. He tried to embezzle money from the company. I assured him that we would work this out as a family. He's in such a deep debt, if we don't help him, he will have to declare bankruptcy. For a man of his social position, nothing is worse than that. We don't want to share his shame either.

FATHER: What do you propose we do?

CLAY: If you give me a signed check, I'll take it over to Uncle David now. He probably needs a few thousand dollars right away just to get back on his feet.

FATHER: Have you always cared so much about David? I haven't noticed.

Pause.

FATHER: I don't give blank checks to anyone. If you want to save David, you should. You are not exactly destitute. You live at home without paying rent. You eat for free. The salary I pay you must be sitting in your bank account. You help him, Clay. Be a good man. (*to WHITE FOX*) I'm sorry to have kept you waiting.

WHITE FOX and FATHER exit.

CLAY: White Fox, whatever you do, Amy is going to die! We all are!

SCENE 17

Amy's room.

WHITE FOX: Here I am. A listener, a healer, a prophet, a sympathizer of your eclipsing soul.

AMY: I don't know you.

WHITE FOX: I know you.

AMY: What do you know?

WHITE FOX: I know that rage lives in your throat.
It's made of ancient things that we manage to
make cloudy. Until the day memories come crisp.

AMY: It's like soaking in a lukewarm swamp.
You can fool yourself for a long
time, but all of a sudden memories come crisp.

WHITE FOX: Take my hand.

AMY: Now you notice it's nothing but slime, thick
with vegetation, green and brown, that you have
been sitting in for years.

WHITE FOX: When you were seven, you played
with magic, and believed it true until winter.
Then the white light revealed nothing but twigs.
You've been suffering ever since.

AMY: Where do I fit in, this cycle of births,
monsters and angels? In this dense bright, my
hands do not deserve to touch the clear sea. But
then where else shall I wash off my red? How can
I go home?

WHITE FOX: I am the messenger of the great
Buddha Amitaba. Do not deviate from the truth.
Believe in my incarnation as medicine. With Lord
Shakyamuni, come home to safety.

As the priest prays, AMY begins screaming.
FATHER comes in when AMY starts screaming,
followed by CLAY.

WHITE FOX: Come to me, all who labor and are
heavy-laden, and I will give you rest.
Take my yoke upon you, and learn from me;
for I am gentle and lowly in heart,
and you will find rest for your souls.
For my yoke is easy, and my burden is light.

AMY: I'm in pain! I'm in pain! I need sharpness
and silence. I need the truth!

Silence.

WHITE FOX: What is the truth?

Pause.

WHITE FOX: You know this. Nothing external
possesses your soul. You have to kill your bastard
child.

FATHER: White Fox!

WHITE FOX: The child is not actual. It is a phantom.

CLAY: Shut the hell up, you phony priest! Stop this charade!

CLAY grabs the WHITE FOX and tries to throw him out of the room. FATHER tries to stop CLAY. WHITE FOX gets out of CLAY's grip.

WHITE FOX: My work is not finished.

CLAY: You don't belong here. You're not family.

WHITE FOX: Amy, if you want me to help you, call me. I will show you the way to live with monsters and angels that you are so afraid of.

AMY: I'm not right.

WHITE FOX: Do not worry. You will recover from this.

CLAY: What is there to recover from? If she isn't pregnant, there is no problem, is there?!

FATHER: Clay, how can you disrespect White Fox?

CLAY: Because I don't believe!

WHITE FOX: Soul raging and homeless.

CLAY: Because I don't believe?

WHITE FOX: No, not because of that. I don't know the reason. I'm sorry I cannot help you. *(turning to AMY)* Winter will be over soon. Underneath the frost of your heart lies sound and color. Try to remember.

WHITE FOX exits.

FATHER: The money she is asking for is for your girlfriend. Amy has been lying to me, hasn't she?

CLAY: I love Rebecca. I want to marry her.

FATHER: Amy is not pregnant then.

CLAY: Duh.

FATHER: Have you no shame? Putting your sister through the agony of deceit and lying viciously about your uncle all for a selfish desire. Who is Rebecca anyway? Who is her family? What is she?

CLAY: She is a student. She goes to the community college.

FATHER: Why do people say she is a prostitute?

CLAY: Who have you been talking to about Rebecca?

FATHER: People talk. It's no longer possible to save our family dignity with you going around with questionable friends and women.

CLAY: I want to know who said that about Rebecca.

FATHER: Are they wrong?

CLAY: I'll kill the motherfucker who said that. I can kill you for repeating it to me. If it was true, I'd have killed *her* already.

FATHER: Stop saying nonsense. Do you have any idea how worried your mother is about your relationship with Rebecca?

CLAY: She can go to hell.

FATHER: Clay!

CLAY: You're wasting your breath trying to make me feel guilty about Mother. I have no use for her right now.

FATHER: What do you want from me then?

CLAY: Money! I want to give Rebecca a certain life style. The money you have was my father's. You took his company. You took his wife. That makes you in debt to me, the rightful owner of the company. I'm blood.

FATHER: The company would have gone down if I didn't take over. Do you really think you deserve what I have built over twenty years?

CLAY: You would have ended your life as a clerk at my father's company if he didn't die. Tell me, when was the first time you fucked my mother? Was it really after the accident?

FATHER: There is nothing good about you, is there?

CLAY: It's a sad story. Anyway, you took things from me. I think you need to give it back.

FATHER: You don't care about the business. Do you think I will allow you to destroy it all for the sake of your little tart?

CLAY: You stupid old fool!

CLAY kicks his father down and stomps all over his body. AMY clings to CLAY.

AMY: Stop! Stop! Are you crazy?

FATHER: Let him, Amy. Let him trample on me to his heart's content.

AMY: He is our father!

CLAY stops, and turns to look at AMY.

CLAY: What does it matter?

AMY: You are a depraved, degenerate human being. And there is no reason for it. You have no right to be so fucked up.

CLAY: Are you any less fucked up than me? Is anyone?

AMY: Yes, Clay! We belong to the human race. Where do you belong, huh? You look at Dad now and tell me that.

CLAY: What are you suggesting?

AMY: That I was wrong about you. You are not my soul, not my brother, not anything but a waste.

CLAY: You betray me in your heart, I will hate you.

AMY: I'm not betraying you. I'm cutting you out of my heart. Obliterated. Demolished. Burnt. Gone.

CLAY slaps AMY. She backs away, but he goes after her. FATHER grabs him. They struggle.

CLAY: You asked for it! This is how I content my heart!

He stomps furiously on his father. MOTHER enters in the midst of the fury.

MOTHER: Henry!

She grabs CLAY's hair and topples him to the floor. She falls on him.

MOTHER: Are you insane?

CLAY: He pushed me to it!

MOTHER: You're the meanest, vilest human being I know. I cannot believe that you came out of my own womb. I don't recognize you. Your soul is blind. You cannot see that with every outrage you cut me, cut my peace, cut my wish, cut my life.

CLAY: Isn't that what you did to my real dad?

MOTHER: What are you talking about?

CLAY: Why did he get into an accident, huh? It wasn't raining, he wasn't drinking. He was a good driver. There was no reason for it except that he wanted to. How did you make him want death, Mom?

AMY: Clay, what are you doing? You don't even mean anything you are saying.

MOTHER: What do you think you know?

CLAY: I think maybe he checked out. And you drove him to it. I wondered about it all my life.

AMY: Liar! You never thought about it before this minute.

CLAY: Shut up! I think we are all guilty. Born guilty. It's in our blood.

MOTHER: Where does this fantasy come from? The accident happened more than twenty years ago. You were five years old. You barely remember him.

AMY: Mom, he doesn't care about any of that. He's just being evil.

MOTHER: Our family is crippled because of you.

CLAY: I don't think I made that happen all by my lonely self.

MOTHER: Look at us, Clay. Just look at all of us.

CLAY: We are the picture of a perfect American family. Just what you always wanted, I'm sure, since you were a little girl.

MOTHER: Get out. You're not staying one minute longer in this house. You are disowned. Get out!

CLAY: I have some rights to this place, this life style. I'm entitled to this life that you dreamt up. It's my birth right.

MOTHER: You renounced it by attacking your father.

AMY: He'll die out there.

MOTHER: *(to AMY)* What do you know about it? Henry, why don't you say something? He has injured and humiliated you. Say something to him.

CLAY: I have nowhere else to go.

MOTHER: Go to that harlot of yours. Stay with her.

CLAY slaps his MOTHER. FATHER flies at him and slaps CLAY hard. A beat. They stare at each other. FATHER slaps him again.

Silence. Stillness.

FATHER: I don't know what force brought us strangers to be father and son. But I have cared for you. Cared for you deeply. Where did I fail?

MOTHER: You exasperate me, Henry. Don't waste your sorrow on him. He is incapable of understanding our language. Get out, Clay. If you don't, I'll call the police.

FATHER: Striking your mother is the last of your destructive acts in this house. You have no lower depth to sink than you've gone today. Get out.

Pause.

CLAY exits. The door slams.

MOTHER: Loving him only harms you.

AMY: Maybe our loving him harmed him somehow.

FATHER: He looks so much like Walter. Sometimes I have to stop myself from calling him by his father's name. Where have you been, Walter? I see him, he is young and strong. I reach over to grab his shoulder, then I realize it's Clay.

SCENE 18

The next day. ANNE enters Amy's room. Evening.

AMY is in bed.

ANNE: How are you?

AMY: Fine.

ANNE: Feeling better?

AMY: I guess.

ANNE: I brought some soup for tomorrow.

AMY: *(sarcastic)* Chicken noodle?

Pause.

ANNE: Your parents were worried sick about you.

AMY: They're my parents.

Pause.

ANNE: I thought we were friends.

AMY: *(sarcastic)* You are the most perfect friend I have.

Pause.

AMY: I'm sorry.

ANNE: What do you think you know about me?

AMY: *(judgmental)* I think you watch the Home Shopping Network.

ANNE: I do that sometimes when I can't sleep. Usually at four in the morning. I scrub the kitchen floor at that hour too.

Pause.

AMY: How do you put yourself to sleep again?

ANNE: I imagine the Milky Way on my ceiling. Stars fall on me, my left shoulder disappears into the white light. I remind myself that in the fabric of history, my blood is water. So I should sleep.

AMY: How many nights like that do you live?

ANNE: Infinite. Only one.

AMY: Even when we were small, Clay was different. He took money out of Mom's purse to buy me silly things. Superman comic books. Sweet rice cakes in March for Hinamatsuri, painted cloth Koinobori in May for the Boys' Day, pink cotton candy on Memorial day, white tree barks that were meant to be burned to guide the ancestors' spirits during Obon in August. I used love the smell of those barks and kept them under my pillow. Every time Mom asked us where we got the money, I would hide behind Clay, but he would look straight into her eyes and say "I found the money on the street."

ANNE: Your mother probably knew and forgave you two.

AMY: Clay knew that all he had to do was ask her for the money. But he didn't.

Pause.

AMY: He wasn't afraid of anything. So I was fearless when I was with him.

ANNE: You love Clay very much.

AMY: He was my hero.

ANNE: He'll come home. It's always possible to start over.

AMY: I don't know if I want him back.

ANNE: You don't have to decide now.

Pause.

ANNE: Are you sleepy?

AMY: Yes.

ANNE: Sweet dreams.

AMY: You too, Anne. Sweet dreams.

SCENE 19

Anne and James' apartment.

JAMES: I'd feel better if you went to see a doctor. How long have you had this headache?

ANNE: It's really nothing to worry about. Because of the snow the girls have cabin fever. They are loud and demanding, which doesn't help my little headache. As soon as the weather is better, I'll get my friend Jane to take them to the park with her kids, so I can have a little silence.

JAMES: I don't know about Jane's kids. They seem a bit aggressive. How old are they?

ANNE: The younger one is eight, same as our Jamie.

JAMES: Which means Sachiko is too young to play with both of them. Their older girl must be ten. Sachiko is only six.

ANNE: I know how old my children are, James. I thought this was about my headache.

JAMES: I'm sorry.

ANNE: I need something of my own. You have your work, the girls have school. I don't have anywhere to go.

JAMES: You wanted to stay home and be a full-time mother, remember? It was your own choice.

ANNE: Maybe I made a mistake.

JAMES: Anne? What's wrong?

ANNE: I don't know. I want to do something with my life.

JAMES: Ok. Let's figure this out. Maybe you'd like to go to graduate school.

ANNE: What will I study?

JAMES: You studied Literature in college. You can continue that.

ANNE: I don't have to go back to school.

JAMES: A job then?

ANNE: Wear panty hoes and ride the rush hour train every day into Manhattan and back?

JAMES: Volunteer work? You could teach reading and writing at the library maybe.

They must have programs for children in need.

Long pause.

ANNE: I want to be here when Jamie and Sachiko get home from school. I want to take a big part in their growing up. I want to be here when you get home from work, too late to tuck the children in bed, the dinner I made already cold. Every morning when I get up, I'm delighted to find you next to me. Delighted to meet my girls again in a new day. But once in a while I truly wish I had made different choices.

JAMES: How long do those moments last?

ANNE: Not long. Only a very small fraction of eternity. Then I come home.

JAMES embraces ANNE.

SCENE 20

The night streets. The same evening. Someone grabs CLAY's arm.

JOE: I've been looking for you, Clay.

CLAY: Joe.

JOE: Where have you been hiding?

CLAY: I was looking for you too.

JOE: Got my money?

CLAY: I'm getting it.

JOE: Better be tonight. Seventeen grand.

CLAY: Seventeen?

JOE: Interest. It's not free money. It's business. And tomorrow morning, you're gonna owe me eighteen. Day after tomorrow, I'm gonna have a talk with you. Day after that, I gotta have a talk with your old man.

CLAY: I know where I can get the money. I'll pay you back tonight.

JOE: Good. And if you need more money tomorrow after paying me back, I'll lend it to you again. But if you don't pay me back, we can't be friends anymore.

CLAY: I understand the contract.

JOE: Before the first siren of an ambulance tears the thin sleep of the city, get the money to me. I'll wait up.

JOE exits.

CLAY: Ten million people in the city. Think. Think.

SCENE 21

JAMES is in his office. Late. He clears his desk and accidentally knocks over a framed picture of ANNE. The glass shatters.

He looks down at the broken frame, and suddenly feels urgent fear.

JAMES: A breathless second of circular motion descending, then a universe is created with a big bang. I stand over the newborn stars. Everything I lost in my life is in this galaxy of a broken likeness of my love.

Pause.

JAMES: Anne!

He grabs the phone and dials. It rings and rings and rings.

SCENE 2

Anne's apartment. The doorbell rings. FATHER enters.

ANNE: Henry. Is everything all right?

FATHER: Have you seen Clay? I thought James might be in touch with my son.

ANNE: I haven't heard anything.

FATHER: If you see him, would you tell him to come home?

ANNE: Of course.

FATHER: I fear at any moment he can be beaten, arrested or die in a ditch somewhere. His behavior has no safety latch. He's free with his idiocy and malice. I fear for his life.

ANNE: He has strayed from the normal orbit of life, but he will get back on course. You'll see.

FATHER: If he shows up, please give him this money. Three thousand dollars. It's the most I can withdraw from our account without making my wife suspicious. This should tie him over until he decides to come home.

The intercom buzzer. ANNE goes to answer it.

ANNE: Henry, it's Elizabeth. She is on her way up, ok?

The doorbell rings. ANNE opens the door to let MOTHER in.

MOTHER: What are you doing here?

FATHER: Hello, Elizabeth.

MOTHER: Is Clay here, Anne?

ANNE: No. He hasn't come.

MOTHER: So you're here to leave the money in case he shows up.

FATHER: He is out there flying without a lifeline.

MOTHER: He cut it himself, Henry. Your generosity poisons his mind.

FATHER: Flying without a lifeline. I'm afraid for his untimely death.

MOTHER: Of a despised life. Come home now. We still have Timothy and Amy. Remember?

FATHER: How can you consider him dead?

MOTHER: Anne, I'm sorry to bother you with our problems. Henry, let's go.

ANNE: Elizabeth, what can I do for you? Why did you come to see me?

Pause.

MOTHER: Perhaps Clay has taught me how to lie. I was going to hide this from Henry.

She gives him an envelope.

MOTHER: I cashed some treasury bills that were in our safety box today. Four thousand dollars. I thought you may not notice it gone. I've become a thief, Henry.

FATHER: No, my dear.

MOTHER: Twenty years. Despite our heartaches over Clay, most of our lives have been music and delight. I fear I have compromised your trust.

FATHER: No, my dear.

MOTHER: For something so abhorrent to come out of my womb, I must bear in myself deep ruin. Many years ago I realized Clay's damage, and I have been afraid of looking into my own soul ever since. A woman warrior will fight her inner fears.

She will conquer the demons of her own heart. The victory is about being whole, so that she can change the world. I have not changed the world. I have not changed Clay. I have spent my life being afraid.

FATHER: No, my dear. You have spent your life weaving ordinary moments of joy and sorrow into our memories so our family can dream about it two, three hundred years from now. You have been brave. Very brave.

MOTHER: Shall we go home?

FATHER: Anne, please give Clay this seven thousand dollars. He may not accept it if he knew it came from us. He may be angry.

ANNE: I'm sure he will appreciate it.

FATHER: It's only money. It won't change him. Even so.

FATHER and MOTHER exit. ANNE stands silent.

SCENE 23

JAMES is in his office.

CO-WORKER: James, aren't you going home? It's late.

JAMES: Soon. I'm trying to finish some things so I can take a long weekend.

CO-WORKER: Are you going somewhere?

JAMES: Taking my family skiing.

CO-WORKER: That's nice. Well, I'm going home.

JAMES: Good night.

Pause.

He continues working. After a while, he begins to clear his desk and gets ready to leave. He knocks over a framed picture of Anne by accident. The glass shatters. He looks down at the broken frame, and suddenly feels urgent fear.

JAMES: In this one second of fracture, everything is possible. I can gain the world or lose everything in it. How can I rewind this second so I am not me at this moment but me a moment before.

Something has pierced my heart, a doubt, a consequence, a fear, of my life lived in distraction.

Pause.

JAMES: Anne!

He grabs the phone and dials. It rings and rings and rings.

SCENE 24

Anne's apartment. The doorbell rings.

CLAY: Hello.

ANNE: Come in, Clay. I was hoping that you'd stop by tonight.

CLAY: Where is James?

ANNE: He's still at work. I have something for you.

CLAY: What?

ANNE: Money. You needed money. Seven thousand dollars.

CLAY: *(showing no joy)* Whose money is it?

ANNE: Don't ask. Just take it.

CLAY: Come on, Anne. Who says just take the money, no string attached, no guilt required. Are you a saint?

ANNE: It's your parents'. They are suffering.

Take their money and do some good. Don't waste your life. Don't waste their love. Do you understand? Do you understand anything?

CLAY: I understand perfectly. From now on, I will be a good son. I'll make you and my parents proud. But right now, this precious money, this gift of their love, is not enough.

ANNE: Clay!

CLAY: I have certain obligations. I'm sure you have credit cards and bank cards and checkbooks and such, don't you? Lend me seventeen thousand dollars.

ANNE: I can't get you that kind of money. Even if I could, I would not do it without talking to James first.

CLAY: If you don't help me, I'll be ruined. I'll have to kill myself. Do you understand, Anne?

ANNE: Why are you so selfish? Why do you torment me? Why do you torment everyone who cares about you?

CLAY: If you care about me, save my life. You have the power.

ANNE: Clay, pull yourself together. What did

you do with so much money? Do you need to pay it all back at once?

CLAY: I needed the money because I didn't want anyone else touching Rebecca. Touching her, touching her, touching her with dirty hands, old hands, rich hands. I needed money to stop that. So first I borrowed two thousand dollars and bought her leather coat. Then I borrowed three thousand dollars to put down on a car. It's like that. I know what's going on. She lies to me all the time. Lies about her beeper and her bra and her heels and her lipsticks. I need money. Because she is mine. She is mine. No one else should touch her. When I can't have her, I drink my own blood, a scorching flame of blue rage.

ANNE: You anguish because you are attached to something that is not real.   It's not too late, Clay. You can give up this suffering. You can go home.

CLAY: You think you know everything and that the everything you know is the right thing.   James with his six-figure job and you, a stay-at-home-wife who goes to the PTA meetings, and two daughters who wear matching dresses. Who cares? The dark night is expanding and collapsing into a universe hostile and stupid. And I couldn't even get Rebecca to dress up on Halloween as death to parade with me to the flat edge of the planet. We should fall off the edge together. Fall a long long way into the unconscious delicious one-thousand-degree never-ending fire of blue hell. My wings are crooked.

Pause.

ANNE: Who should fall off the edge? You and Rebecca? Or you and me?

CLAY: You won't help me, will you?

ANNE: I'm trying.

CLAY: I need you.

ANNE: I'm here.

Long pause.

CLAY: Can I have a cup of tea?

Pause.

CLAY: You are right. I'm sorry. I won't ask you anymore.

They look into each other's eyes. CLAY smiles. He sits down.

CLAY: I'm thirsty.

ANNE turns her back to him to go to the kitchen to make tea. She takes off her rings to wash her hands. After drying her hands with a towel, she puts the rings back on. CLAY watches.

ANNE: I'll talk to James and see what we can do. He cares about you a great deal.

CLAY stands up. As he approaches ANNE from behind, he picks up a large kitchen knife. He hides the knife behind his back. She turns around and sees his menacing expression.

ANNE: What do you want?

CLAY: Nothing.

CLAY advances on ANNE.

ANNE: Stay there.

CLAY: Why are you scared?

They circle each other.

ANNE: Clay, it's me.

CLAY: I know who you are.

She steps backwards, trying to get away from CLAY. He follows her. This goes on in silence for a quite a while. Finally CLAY jumps on her and restrains her. She screams.

CLAY: Shut up, bitch.

ANNE: Are you insane?

CLAY: Aren't we all? You think your little life is sane and safe? The hell is right around the corner, and you conjured me, your demon from the depth of darkness. You're the insane one.

ANNE: I did not. This is all your making.

CLAY: You're my partner in crime.

ANNE: Never.

CLAY: Don't argue with me. You know where you are going, don't you?

ANNE: How would you face James?

CLAY: Don't worry about me.

ANNE: I have children. You know them. You know my children. They are sleeping in their bedroom.

CLAY: Well then, you better be quiet not to wake them up.

ANNE: They need me. I don't want to die.

CLAY: I'm sure you don't. It's natural.

ANNE: Please.

CLAY: But I need the money. I know you have expensive jewelry. For every anniversary, birthday, Christmas, James has given you something that sparkles on you. Isn't that right? Because he loves you so much.

ANNE: Take it. Take anything you want except my life.

CLAY: It's too late now. After a certain point, there is no way back home.

ANNE breaks free from him and tries to get away. He grabs after her. They struggle. She picks up a cushion and swings it at him. The knife cuts in to the cushion and red feathers fly all over the room. She trips and falls. They are both covered in feathers.

ANNE: Help! Help!

CLAY grabs her.

ANNE: No, no no. Don't! Don't! Save me. Save me. James!

He cuts her throat.

CLAY: Die quickly, Anne.

He pulls her to him and slashes her body from right to left, down to her waist, then lets go of her limp body. Long pause.

CLAY: God, look on this your servant, lying in great weakness, and comfort her with the promise of life ever-lasting, given in the resurrection of your Son Jesus Christ our Lord.

He stands over her body as the shadows deepen in the room. He shudders suddenly. His knees buckle as he tries to move. He goes through her things and gets what he wanted.

CLAY: I'm free. I've left home behind, left sanity behind, left behind the chance I had to end peacefully this story that is my life. There is nothing to go back to, nothing to live for, nothing to prove. I am free.

For the blood I shed, one day I will be caught in a cycle, beginningless and endless, to live forever, to suffer eternally in the flickering blazing hell. But that's a far away future. My luck in this world is just beginning.

As he makes his getaway, he slips and slides in Anne's blood.

The phone starts ringing. It rings and rings and rings.

End of Play

Afterword

"My luck in this world is just beginning." The last line of Chiori Miyagawa's *Woman Killer* appears verbatim in Donald Keene's translation of Chikamatsu's eighteenth-century play, *The Woman-Killer and the Hell of Oil*. This intact sentence from the play that inspired her 2001 work illuminates the force of Miyagawa's work, its jarring historical and cultural discontinuities, its mixture of brutality and beauty, its disorienting verbal and visual impact.

Miyagawa adamantly refuses to provide those signposts that more comforting dramatists leave to reassure audiences. And her departure from Chikamatsu's conclusion is exemplary here. When Yohei, the anti-hero of the earlier play, reassures himself about his luck, there is reason to suspect that it may be more bad than good, and soon, indeed, a group of men drag him to his execution. Chikamatsu concludes with this wild justice and with the narrator's promise that Yohei's reputation is ruined forever. Miyagawa's play stages the murder and then — ends. We cannot know what happens to Clay. The phone rings, and that's all.

That ringing phone signals Miyagawa's dramaturgical brilliance. The knifed cushion and the storm of red feathers; the terrible stabbing; the Christian invocation; Clay's declaration of freedom; finally, echoing the endings of the two previous scenes, the sound of that ringing phone: Miyagawa offers no key to this sequence, no apology for the violence, no wink about the prayer, no promise of distance from Clay's final, proud declaration.

The conflicting layers of this final scene typify *Woman Killer*. So often, theatrical appropriation turns everything it touches into yet another ironic commodity; such ironic appropriation can be funny, even critically acute, but it can also produce a dull sensation of sameness. When a playwright or production produces a comfortable distance from unfamiliar things for the audience, the audience can feel the relief of knowing that it does not really have to engage with the promise or challenge or threat of strangeness. That strangeness will evanesce, or, more often, there will never be a chance for strangeness at all: whatever could have been inassimilable has been packaged for us.

Miyagawa's work, line by line and moment by moment, refuses such assimilation. Take the scene where Clay encounters Rebecca in front of a nightclub. Having beaten up her date, who flees, Clay notices Rebecca's dress:

> CLAY: That's a nice dress. Did he buy it for you?

REBECCA: No, I put it on my Amex. Didn't you promise me a dress for New Year?

CLAY: When I thought you were coming out with me tonight.

REBECCA: Here I am.

CLAY: What do you want from me?

REBECCA: A silk kimono in red chrysanthemum patterns that I can wear with a sash on high waist like the courtesans of Tennoji House.

CLAY: Tennoji House?

REBECCA: Come on, I know you've been there. On 42nd Street off the Tokaido path.

The trickiest part of this passage might be the last of Clay's questions. On the one hand, he speaks for a large part of a disconcerted audience: "Tennoji House?" Tennoji House, here, in New York, where Amex can buy anything? It becomes clear, however, that Clay's question, rather than a sign that he shares the audience's bewilderment, is a defensive gesture, meant to hide knowledge of a place he would like to pretend he does now know.

This is a New York where 42nd Street intersects with the grand Tokaido path. He and Rebecca, that is, live in the same city.

The audience of *Woman Killer*, then, may experience as discontinuity that same metropolis in which its characters live their everyday lives. This palimpsest of Japan and New York, this world where the priest of the fox god makes house calls in Brooklyn, is very different from many other works about crossing or living between cultures. If the more common theatrical strategy is to stage the clash of cultures as a theme within a play, Miyagawa makes newly vivid the existence between cultures — and across historical periods — precisely by her ingenious refusal to mark this clash as a clash. It is, so to speak, audiences who produce the clash by taking apart the elements that the playwright has sutured together: Tennoji House is not to be found in New York, 42nd Street does not intersect with the Tokaido path.

The palimpsest of cultures here is not only geographical; it is also historical. The paradox of Clay, as his name suggest, is that he is at once "homeless," unmoored, and intensely skeptical — the readiest, for instance, to deny the priest's authority — and the most deeply subject to an ethics of dignity and damnation that might seem more at home in Chikamatsu's eighteenth-century Japan than in the New York of the early twenty-first. *Woman Killer* lacks Chikamatsu's moralizing conclusion, but nevertheless the force of the ethical and religious beliefs that informs the earlier play remains palpable in Miyagawa's appropriation of it.

This seeming disjunction between a putatively outmoded ethical code and the freedom of the modern metropolis may be the source of Miyagawa's deepest claims on her audience. The play's finale startlingly frames its act of violence in a sequence of Christian and Buddhist beliefs: Clay perversely offers a prayer to Christ for the woman he has murdered and then imagines his eternal reincarnation "in the flickering blazing hell." Can the audience follow Clay in living both these languages simultaneously? Is one or are both of these invocations parodic or empty?

Woman Killer disorients its audience. If we believe we have disentangled New York from Japan, what city is left? Miyagawa's refusal to judge leaves the audience at a loss, wondering about how it habitually responds. What if we don't *know* why something is horrifying?

Martin Harries
New York University

Notes on Contributors

Martin Harries is Professor of English at New York University, where he teaches courses on theater, modernism, and theory. He is the author of two books: *Forgetting Lot's Wife: On Destructive Spectatorship* (Fordham University Press, 2007) and *Scare Quotes from Shakespeare: Marx, Keynes, and the Language of Re-enchantment* (Stanford University Press, 2000). His essays and reviews have appeared in *New German Critique, The Yale Journal of Criticism, Modern Drama, Theatre Journal, TDR, The Hunter On-Line Theater Review, The Village Voice,* and elsewhere. He is at work on a book on theater and mass culture, for which he received a Burkhardt fellowship from the American Council of Learned Societies for 2008-09, when he was a fellow in residence at the Radcliffe Institute for Advanced Study.

Sharon Friedman is an Associate Professor in the Gallatin School of New York University. Her essays have appeared in such publications as *American Studies, New Theatre Quarterly, Women and Performance, Contemporary Authors Bibliographical Series: American Dramatists, TDR, Susan Glaspell: Essays on Her Theater and Fiction* (ed. Ben-Zvi, U. of Michigan Press, 1995), and *Codifying the National Self: Spectators, Actors, and the American Text* (eds. Ozieblo and Narbona, Brussels, P.I.E.

Peter Lang, 2005). She co-directed a New York University Humanities Council Seminar and Conference on "An Interdisciplinary and Intercultural Examination of Twentieth-Century Adaptations and Revisions of Classic Texts" that brought together theatre artists, classicists and performance studies scholars. Her most recent publication is an edited volume entitled, *Feminist Theatrical Revisions of Classic Works* (McFarland, 2009).

Chiori Miyagawa is a Japanese-born, American playwright. Her plays include *I Have Been to Hiroshima Mon Amour* (Voice&Vision at Ohio Theatre, part of The Hiroshima Project 2009); *America Dreaming* commissioned by Music-Theatre Group which premiered at Vineyard Theatre featuring original music by Tan Dun, choreographed by Doug Varone, directed by Michael Mayer(published in Global Foreigners Seagull Books); *Comet Hunter*, a play based on the life of the first woman astronomer, Caroline Herschel (Ensemble Studio Theatre/ Alfred Sloan Science and Technology Commission, *Nothing Forever* and *Yesterday's Window* (both at New York Theatre Workshop, directed by Karin Coonrod, *Nothing* at HERE by New Georges, *Nothing* published in Positive/Negative Women, *Yesterday* published in TAKE TEN), *Woman Killer* (Crossing Jamaica Avenue in co-production with HERE, published in Plays and Playwrights 2002), *Leaving*

Eden (The Meadows School of the Arts, SMU Commission, directed by Greg Leaming), *Awakening* (Performance Space 122 in co-presentation by Dance Theater Workshop and Crossing Jamaica Avenue), *Red Again/Antigone Project* (Women's Project), *Jamaica Avenue* (New York International Fringe Festival, published in Tokens? The NYC Asian American Experiences on Stage), *FireDance* (Voice&Vision), *Broken Morning* (Dallas Theater Center and Crossing Jamaica Avenue at HERE), *Antigone's Red* (Virginia Tech, published in TAKE TEN II.) A collection of her plays, *Thousand Years Waiting and Other Plays*, is forthcoming from Seagull Books as part of an international play series, *In Performance*, for which Carol Martin is the general editor. Chiori has been awarded many grants and fellowships including the New York Foundation for the Arts Playwriting Fellowship, McKnight Playwriting Fellowship, Van Lier Playwriting Fellowship, and Asian Cultural Council Fellowship Rockefeller Bellagio Residency, and Radcliffe Advanced Studies Fellowship at Harvard University.

More titles from NoPassport Press

Antigone Project: A Play in Five Parts
by Tanya Barfield, Karen Hartman, Chiori Miyagawa, Lynn Nottage and
Caridad Svich, with preface by Lisa Schlesinger, introduction by Marianne
McDonald; **ISBN 978-0-578-03150-7**

Amparo Garcia-Crow: The South Texas Plays
(Cocks Have Claws and Wings to Fly, Under a Western Sky, The Faraway Nearby,
Esmeralda Blue) **Preface by Octavio Solis**
ISBN: 978-0-578-01913-0

Anne Garcia-Romero: Collected Plays
(Earthquake Chica, Santa Concepcion, Mary Peabody in Cuba)
Preface by Juliette Carrillo
ISBN: 978-0-6151-8888-1

John Jesurun: Deep Sleep, White Water, Black Maria –
A Media Trilogy **Preface by Fiona Templeton**
ISBN: 978-0-578-02602-2

Lorca: Six Major Plays
(Blood Wedding, Dona Rosita, The House of Bernarda Alba, The Public, The
Shoemaker's Prodigious Wife, Yerma)
In new translations by Caridad Svich, Preface by James Leverett,
introduction by Amy Rogoway;
ISBN: 978-0-578-00221-7

Matthew Maguire: Three Plays
(The Tower, Luscious Music, The Desert) **Preface by Naomi Wallace; ISBN:**
978-0-578-00856-1

Oliver Mayer: Collected Plays
(Conjunto, Joe Louis Blues, Ragged Time) **Preface by Luis Alfaro, Introduction**
by Jon D. Rossini;
ISBN: 978-0-6151-8370-1

Alejandro Morales: Collected Plays
(expat/inferno, marea, Sebastian);
ISBN: 978-0-6151-8621-4

12 Ophelias (a play with broken songs) by Caridad Svich
ISBN: 978-0-6152-4918-6

NoPassport is a sponsored project of Fractured Atlas, a non-profit arts service organization. Contributions in behalf of [Caridad Svich & NoPassport] may be made payable to Fractured Atlas and are tax-deductible to the extent permitted by law.

For online donations go directly to
https://www.fracturedatlas.org/donate/2623

www.ingramcontent.com/pod-product-compliance
Lightning Source LLC
Chambersburg PA
CBHW030345030726
47499CB00003B/912